SEASONS OF SWANS

for Laura and Richard

The author gratefully thanks John Fair and David Wheeler of
the Abbotsbury Swannery in Dorset, England, for generously
helping and for sharing their insight and knowledge.

Copyright © 1990 by Monica Wellington

Library of Congress Cataloging-in-Publication Data
Wellington, Monica.
Seasons of swans/Monica Wellington.—1st ed.
p.   cm.
Summary: The two swans who live on Willow Pond build a nest,
raise a family of little swans, and survive another season.
ISBN 0-525-44621-4
1. Swans—Juvenile fiction.   [1. Swans—Fiction.]   I. Title.
PZ10.3.W458Se   1990
[E]—dc20   89-28893   CIP   AC

Published in the United States by Dutton Children's Books,
a division of Penguin Books USA Inc.
Designer: Martha Rago
Printed in Hong Kong by South China Printing Co.
First Edition   10 9 8 7 6 5 4 3 2 1

SEASONS OF SWANS

Monica Wellington

Dutton Children's Books
New York

Two swans live on Willow Pond.

Together they glide on glassy water.

One swan is a male.
The other is a female.
Every spring they go
to a quiet island
in the pond and
build a strong nest.

There mother swan lays her eggs. Then she flutters and shuffles and settles down gently on them.

She tends the nest and keeps the eggs warm while father swan stays on guard close by. More than a month passes. Finally the eggs are ready to hatch.

First peeping sounds come from inside the eggs. Then they crack, and the babies peck and push their way out.

They quickly wiggle dry.
Now there are six fluffy
baby swans in the nest.

Baby swans are called cygnets.
By the next day, the cygnets
are ready for their first swim.
The parents lead them
to the water.

The family stays close together. Some cygnets swim, while others feel safer riding on their mother's back.

As spring turns to summer, the cygnets grow. They learn to find their favorite waterweeds to eat.

In the dark, a dog sneaks toward the pond. The parents hiss and flap their wings to chase the dog away. Swans will be fierce to keep their cygnets safe.

The hot summer murmurs
with insects. The cygnets'
necks grow long. Stiff
feathers grow over their
soft down. The young
swans will soon be
ready to fly.

By the time the cool
autumn winds rustle,
the young swans' wings
have grown strong.
The changing season calls
one swan into the sky.

The air turns crisp and brisk.
More young swans fly away.
Only one remains with its
parents at Willow Pond, a
place of mild winters.

Through the soft slow winter days, the children bring bread and grains to the swans. They are hungry and eager for the food.

On a sparkling day when
the snow has melted, the
last young swan opens
its wings and flies to
join other young swans.
Soon their feathers will
all turn white.

The two swans are by themselves again. The wind whispers soft sounds. A new spring is coming to Willow Pond.